TRiM
Helps Out

Written by
Deborah Hopkinson

Illustrated by
Kristy Caldwell

PEACHTREE
ATLANTA

For the brave people of Ukraine and their beloved
pets, especially Xenta and her "little horses."

—D. H.

For Judy and Scott Caldwell.
We're making it happen.

—K. C.

Published by
PEACHTREE PUBLISHING COMPANY INC.
1700 Chattahoochee Avenue
Atlanta, Georgia 30318-2112
PeachtreeBooks.com

Text © 2023 by Deborah Hopkinson
Illustrations © 2023 by Kristy Caldwell

Edited Kathy Landwehr
Design and composition by Lily Steele

The illustrations were rendered digitally.
Photo of Trim and Matthew Flinders, Port Lincoln, South Australia
Camloo, CC BY-SA 4.0 *https://creativecommons.org/licenses/by-sa/4.0,*
via Wikimedia Commons

Printed and bound in June 2023 at R.R. Donnelley, Dongguan, China.
10 9 8 7 6 5 4 3 2 1
First Edition
ISBN: 978-1-68263-291-8

Library of Congress Cataloging-in-Publication Data

Names: Hopkinson, Deborah, author. | Caldwell, Kristy, illustrator.
Title: Trim helps out / written by Deborah Hopkinson ; illustrated by Kristy Caldwell.
Description: First edition. | Atlanta, Georgia : Peachtree Publishing Company Inc., 2023. | Series: Trim ; 2 |
Audience: Ages 7–10. | Audience: Grades 2–3. | Summary: On his first morning at sea, ship's cat Trim looks
for ways to help out, and makes a new friend along the way.
Identifiers: LCCN 2023012919 | ISBN 9781682632918 (hardcover) | ISBN 9781682634448 (ebook)
Subjects: CYAC: Cats—Fiction. | Animals—Fiction. | Friendship—Fiction. | Sailing ships—Fiction. |
LCGFT: Animal fiction.
Classification: LCC PZ7.H778125 Tr 2023 | DDC [Fic]—dc23
LC record available at *https://lccn.loc.gov/2023012919*

Contents

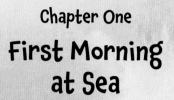

Chapter One
First Morning at Sea

Trim was a brand-new ship's cat.

It was his first morning at sea.

He wanted to do a good job.

But Trim wondered, *How can I help?*

Everyone seemed so busy.

Captain Flinders stood at the helm,
steering the big, fine ship.

Cook was in the galley making nice,
warm biscuits.

Will was high in the crow's nest,

painting the sea and sky.

The gardener was watering plants in

the greenhouse.

The nature artist was drawing a flower.

And the naturalist was working on
the collection.

Penny was helping the sailors with the ropes.

Everyone has an important job, Trim thought. *What about me?*

Trim went to find Jack. The ship's parrot was sure to know what a cat should do.

Chapter Two
Trim Gets His First Job

"Jack, I want to help out," Trim said. "What should I do?"

"A ship's cat should patrol the hold," Jack said. "Everyone knows that."

"Oh," said Trim, who did *not* know. "What's the hold?"

"It's where we store fresh water to drink and flour for biscuits," Jack said. "It's down here."

"It's dark down there," Trim said.

10

"That's why it's your job to patrol the hold," Jack said. "Cats can see in the dark."

"What does 'patrol' mean?" Trim asked.

"It means to look around very carefully," Jack said.

"What should I look for?" Trim asked.

"Rats, of course!" Jack squawked. "You don't want creepy, scary-looking rats biting us or eating our food, do you?"

"I guess not," Trim said. "But what do rats look—"

Before Trim could finish, Jack flew off to find some snacks.

The hold was dark and full of shadows.

Trim saw barrels of oatmeal and flour.

He saw casks of fresh water.

He saw crates piled with coconuts.

Trim did not see any creepy, scary-looking rats.

Trim wasn't even sure he *wanted* to see a creepy, scary-looking rat.

What if it tried to bite him?

But Trim had made up his mind to be a good ship's cat. So he set out to patrol the hold anyway.

Trim lifted one paw and put it down.

Trim lifted another paw and put it down.

Suddenly a voice rang out. "Who are you?"

Trim was so scared he leaped high into
the air.

And because he was a cat, he landed on
all four paws. PLOP!

"Well, who are you?" the stranger demanded.

"I'm Trim, the new ship's cat," Trim said. "What's your name?"

"I am Princess Beatrix. You can call me Princess Bea," she said. "What are you doing in the hold?"

"I'm on patrol," Trim said. "I'm watching out for creepy, scary-looking rats so they don't bite us or eat our food."

"Oh, I patrol the hold," Princess Bea said. "That's *my* job."

Trim sighed. All the jobs were taken! "Then what should I do?" he asked.

"I have a more important job for you. Bring me one of Cook's nice, warm biscuits," Princess Bea commanded. "I'm hungry from being on patrol."

"I can do that!" Trim said. "I can do that job very well."

Trim felt happy. He definitely knew more about biscuits than he did about rats.

Chapter Three
Trim's More
Important Job

Trim dashed out of the hold, across the deck, and into the galley.

He rubbed against Cook's leg. *"Mew! Mew!"*

"Hungry again, Trim?" Cook laughed. "Here you go."

Trim rushed back to the hold, carrying a nice, warm biscuit in his mouth.

Jack swooped down and asked, "Why aren't you doing your job?"

Trim put the biscuit on the deck. "I'm doing a more important job now," he said. "I'm helping my new friend."

"You met a new friend?" Jack asked.

"Yes, she's called Princess Bea," Trim said. "She said it's her job to patrol the hold. I'm helping out by bringing her a biscuit."

"*Hmmm*," Jack said. "Tell me, does your new friend have gray fur and pink feet?"

Trim nodded.

"Does she have black eyes and a long skinny tail?"

Trim nodded again.

"Silly kitten!" Jack squawked. "Don't you know, Princess Bea is a . . ."

27

Before Jack could finish, a creepy,
scary-looking creature scuttled across
the deck.

It headed straight for Penny, who had
curled up for her morning nap.

Oh, no! thought Trim. *A rat is about to
bite Penny!*

Chapter Four
Charge!

"Wake up, Penny!" Trim yelled.

But Penny kept snoozing.

Trim looked around. What should he do?

Suddenly, Princess Bea raced out of the hold. "Follow me, Trim!" she shouted. "Charge!"

31

Princess Bea charged.

Trim charged too.

They chased the creepy, scary-looking creature into a corner.

"Good job, Trim," Princess Bea said.

Then she ran back to the hold.

Trim was alone with the creepy,
scary-looking creature. But not for long.

Captain Flinders ran over, scooped the creature up in a small box, and closed the lid.

"What a brave kitten you are, my boy!" he said.

Will took the box. "This must have escaped from our nature collection."

Trim wasn't sure why there were rats in the nature collection. But he hoped the creepy, scary-looking creature wouldn't bite Will.

Trim clambered up to Captain Flinders'
shoulder. He would keep the captain
company for the rest of the day. That seemed
like an important job for a ship's cat.

Trim looked down and spied Princess
Bea peering out of the hold.

She winked, then she disappeared into
the darkness below.

The biscuit was nowhere to be seen.

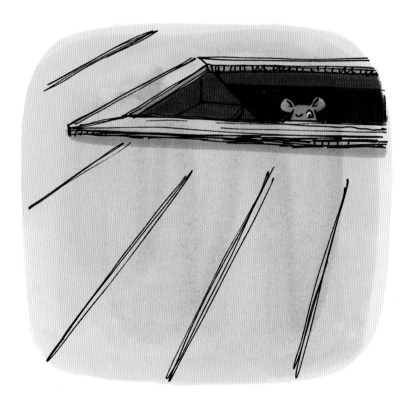

Chapter Five
Four Friends

Later that night, a bright round moon hung in the sky.

Three friends gazed out at the sea.

A soft voice broke the stillness.

"Good evening, I'm Princess Bea." She dropped the biscuit on the deck. "I brought this to share. Can we all be friends?"

"Fine with me," Jack said. "You and Trim did a great job today."

39

"It's fine with me too," Penny said. "Thank you, Princess Bea and Trim. I'm glad you saved me from that scorpion. Their stings hurt."

"Wait!" Trim cried. "The creepy, scary-looking creature was a *scorpion*?"

"All eight legs of it," Jack said with a shudder.

"We have lots of creepy, scary-looking creatures in the nature collection," Penny added. "That's because we're exploring the world to learn new things."

"But . . . but if that was a scorpion, what is a rat?" Trim asked.

Princess Bea cleared her throat. "I'm a rat."

"You're a rat? Do you bite us and eat our food?" Trim asked.

"I promise not to do that," Princess Bea said. "But I will patrol the hold and make sure the supplies are safe."

"Great! And I promise to bring you biscuits," Trim said. "Because helping my friends is a good job for me."

"Thank you, Trim," Princess Bea said.

"You're becoming a fine ship's cat," Penny said.

"Now let's eat!" Jack squawked.

Captain Flinders came to the bow.

Trim perched on his shoulder, right where he belonged.

They watched the stars slide over the great, vast sea.

Trim knew he still had a lot to learn.

But he would always try to be the best ship's cat who ever lived.

And he was.

TRIM HELPS OUT is a made-up story about a real cat who lived in the past. We call this kind of story historical fiction.

Trim was born in 1799. Trim's owner was British explorer Matthew Flinders (1774–1814), captain of the HMS *Investigator*. As part of an expedition between 1801 and 1803, Trim became the first cat to sail around the continent of Australia.

Just as in our story, the crew of the HMS *Investigator* included a naturalist, a gardener, and artists. Will was inspired by landscape painter William Westall, who was only nineteen. Captain Flinders' wife, Ann, wanted to go along, but the Royal Navy wouldn't let her because she was a woman. Matthew and Ann Flinders had one daughter, Anne, who wrote a book about Egyptian mythology. Her son became an explorer too—he journeyed to Egypt as an archaeologist.

Captain Flinders told many funny stories about his beloved cat and called him a "fearless seaman." His tribute to Trim was written in 1809 but was lost until 1971. Today there are statues of these two good friends in England and Australia. And now you know about Trim too.

Matthew Flinders wanted to explore the world because he loved reading sea adventures when he was young. I'll read this story to my cat, Beatrix. I just hope she doesn't decide to run away to sea!

What adventures will you have and write about?

Set Sail with TRIM!

HC: 978-1-68263-291-8

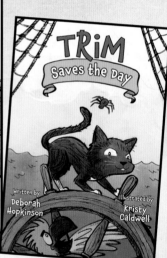

HC: 978-1-68263-290-1

HC: 978-1-68263-293-2